Care Bears

Good Luck Bear's Special Day

By Sonia Sander
Illustrated by Jay Johnson

ISBN-13 978-0-439-88858-5
ISBN-10- 0-439-88858-1
CARE BEARS™ © 2007 Those Characters From Cleveland, Inc.
Used under license by Scholastic Inc. All rights reserved. Published by Scholastic Inc.
SCHOLASTIC and associated logos are trademarks and/or registered trademarks of Scholastic Inc.
12 11 10 9 8 7 6 5 4 3 2 1   7 8 9 10 11/0
Printed in the U.S.A.
First printing, March 2007

SCHOLASTIC INC.
New York   Toronto   London   Auckland   Sydney
Mexico City   New Delhi   Hong Kong   Buenos Aires

Good Luck Bear was working in his garden. He spotted a four-leaf clover.

"I'll have extra good luck today!" he said to himself as he plucked it from the ground.

"Hi, Good Luck Bear!" called out Cheer Bear. "Isn't it a great day?"

"It sure is!" said Good Luck Bear. "Look what I found!"

Just then, rain burst from the sky. Cheer Bear and Good Luck Bear ran for shelter.

The rain didn't last long and when it stopped, it left behind a bright, colorful surprise.

"That's the biggest rainbow I have ever seen!" cried Good Luck Bear.
"Let's follow it and find out where it ends!" said Cheer Bear.

Good Luck Bear spotted his friends Share Bear and Wish Bear.
"Come along on a rainbow adventure with us," called Good Luck Bear.
"That sounds like fun!" said Share Bear.

All of a sudden, a big gust of wind picked up Good Luck Bear's four-leaf clover and blew it away.

"Quick! Let's chase after it!" cried Cheer Bear.

Soon, more of their friends gathered to see what was happening. "Come quickly," called out Wish Bear. "We're chasing Good Luck Bear's four-leaf clover to the end of the rainbow."

"It's no use," cried Good Luck Bear. "We'll never catch it!"

"Maybe the wind will get tired of blowing your four-leaf clover soon," added Funshine Bear.

"Follow me, I've almost got it!" exclaimed Cheer Bear.

Soon, the friends came to a dandelion patch.

Wish Bear picked a dandelion and handed it to Good Luck Bear.

"You should make a wish," she suggested.

"I wish I could catch my four-leaf clover," said Good Luck Bear. They blew on the dandelion for extra luck.

The Care Bears kept chasing the four-leaf clover until they came to a field. It was entirely full of four-leaf clovers.

"We've found enough four-leaf clovers for everyone!" cried Friend Bear.

"And look, there's the end of the rainbow!" cried Cheer Bear.

When they got to the end of the rainbow, Good Luck Bear's four-leaf clover was waiting there. So was a huge golden pot of yummy rainbow bars. "What a lucky surprise!" exclaimed Champ Bear.

Good Luck Bear and Cheer Bear passed out all of the rainbow bars.

Good Luck Bear and Cheer Bear passed out all of
the rainbow bars.

"Thank you for inviting us to share your rainbow adventure," said Share Bear and Harmony Bear.

"I can't think of a better way to spend the day," added Love-a-lot Bear.

"Today started out as a special day for me," said Good Luck Bear.
"But it turned out to be a lucky day for all of us!"